The Messy Monkey Tea Party

Illustrated by Christina Genth
Written by Cheri Bivin Deich

red cygnet™ PRESS

San Diego, California

red
cygnet™
PRESS

---

*I would like to dedicate the book to my wonderful family and
in loving memory of my mother Nan.– CG*

I am dedicating this book to Matt, Elle, Jonah, and Chloe. – CBD

Illustrations copyright © 2007 Christina Genth
Manuscript copyright © 2007 Cheri Bivin Deich
Book copyright © 2007 Red Cygnet Press, Inc., 11858 Stoney Peak Dr. #525, San Diego, CA 92128

Cover and book design: Amy Stirnkorb

First Edition 2007
10 9 8 7 6 5 4 3 2
Printed in China

Library of Congress Cataloging-in-Publication Data

Deich, Cheri Bivin.
The messy monkey tea party / written by Cheri Bivin Deich ; illustrated by Christina Genth. -- 1st ed.
p. cm.
Summary: A great mess ensues when a child invites the zoo animals to come for tea.
ISBN-13: 978-1-60108-006-6 (hardcover)
ISBN-10: 1-60108-006-9 (hardcover)
[1. Zoo animals--Fiction. 2. Tea--Fiction. 3. Parties--Fiction.
4. Stories in rhyme.] I. Genth, Christina, ill. II. Title.
PZ8.3.D3648Me 2007
[E]--dc22
2006017488

I was alone with nothing to do
So I decided to take a trip to the zoo.

But then I thought of a brilliant plan
And so my wonderful adventure began.

I wrote invitations
For a zoo animal tea,
I said to bring one friend,
Two, even three.

The invitations were written
In great detail
And were soon picked up
With the morning mail.

The next thing I knew,
It was three days later,
And I was seated
With two alligators.

The first tried to sit
And got her tail stuck.
The second requested
A serving of duck.

It became obvious my plan
Would simply not work
When the tail-stuck gator
Went completely berserk.

I freed her tail as quickly as I could
And asked them both nicely
To leave if they would.

The two of them slowly crawled right away,
I was glad I did not ask them to stay.

My next guest to arrive, I did not understand,
He immediately plunged his head in the sand.

I had heard the ostrich can be terribly shy,
But I had hoped he'd at least come out to say, "Hi!"

The hippos came next to have tea and some cake.
This, too, was a somewhat enormous mistake.

Three hippos had come in outstanding attire,
But their smell was quite bad since
They lounge in the mire.

Their appetites were almost as big as themselves,
They ate most of the food I had stored on the shelves!

Something must have scared them, and they left with a thunder...

... When out hopped two joeys!
(They came from down under.)

The joeys were polite and as kind as could be,
They quietly sat as they sipped on their tea.

But soon they were off with a bounce and a bound,
They jumped over the fence without making a sound.

An elephant arrived in her scarf and her hat,
And she made a huge scene when she spotted a rat.

She jumped up on a chair and shrieked ever so loud,
As she trumpeted upward, she parted a cloud.

As the rat ran away,
She stepped down from the chair,
(But she wasn't convinced
That the rat wasn't there.)

She drank her tea nervously
And then said, "Good-bye."

(Rats freak out elephants,
I don't really know why)

buzz!

buzz!

A bear with two cubs came next and sat down,
The mother was wearing an awfully big frown.

I said, "Your bear nose looks bright red to me."
"Of course," she cried. "I've been stung by a bee!"

"I wanted to bring honey to put in our tea,
When a huge angry swarm flew out from the tree."

"Don't worry," she said, "they didn't follow me here."
Then all of a sudden bees began to appear.

They buzzed hurriedly round our little tea table,
We ran for shelter, fast as we were able.

Now this was beginning to be just too much.
Have you ever even heard of a tale that is such?

An alligator stuck.
One wants to eat duck.

The ostrich with its head in the ground.
The hippos that made the thundering sound.

The kangaroos bouncing in and out just like that.
The two-ton elephant afraid of a rat.

And those bears with the bees
Swarming down from the trees!

I hadn't thought the tea party would be such a mess
when up came five monkeys all wearing one dress.

Heads poked from each sleeve,
Three heads from the neck.
It was then I became a real nervous wreck!

They swung from the trees and tossed dishes around
And were making a constant, low chattering sound.

They threw cake and their cookies this way and that
Then plopped in a chair and finally sat.

Those monkeys began tying napkins in knots
On their heads they balanced cups and tea pots.

I had taken about all I could bear
When the clock struck three,
There was no time to spare.

I told those monkeys to go back to the zoo.
"Now go away. Go. Just Go away. Shooo!"

I pulled the ostrich's head from out of the sand,
And sent him a packin' with the five-monkey band.

Now I had to hurry and
Have everything clean,
My mom would be home by 3:15!
It was the Biggest Mess I had ever seen!

Now, I've made some messes gigantic before,
But when I looked over my wet bedroom floor,

I had to be fast and I had to be quick,
I had to get rid of the smell and the ick!

First I cleaned up the hippo's brown goo,
Then it was off to the next mess I flew.

I fixed the elephant's chair
With some tape and some glue
(It's amazing what some tape
And some good glue can do.)

The ostrich's sand I swept into a pan
Then I swept up the path
Where the bears and I ran.

The alligators were fine,
        they were just pests,
        The kangaroos had been
The most polite of the guests.

By far the messiest were the monkeys, you see,
There's a reason you don't ask animals to tea!

By the end of the day, I was one tired child,
Zoo animals and my imagination both had run Wild!